To my mom

Hazel and Twig
THE
LOST EGG

Brenna Burns Yu

CANDLEWICK PRESS

HAZEL and her little sister, Twig, were sitting on a rock in the meadow. Hazel was making a wildflower chain. Twig was unmaking the wildflower chain.

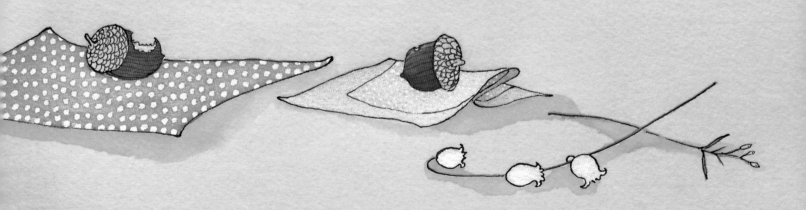

Hazel said, "Twig, you will have to find your own rock!"

So Twig did.

But the rock was not a rock. It was an egg.

Hazel said, "I know! Let's hatch it together." So they sat on the egg to keep it warm.

But an egg takes a very long time to hatch. . . .

And when it started to rain, they couldn't wait any longer.
"Come on, little egg!" said Hazel. "You'll like living with us."

Twig cheered.

"Umma and Appa will be so happy that we are bringing home an egg," Hazel said.

Then they heard their father calling.

"Hazel! Twig!" Appa said. "I was worried that you were lost.
The rain is falling very hard."

"We are not lost!" Hazel said. "We are bringing home an egg."

"Oh my," Appa said. "But why is Twig sitting on top of it?"

"To keep it warm until it hatches," Hazel replied.

"Of course," Appa said.

"You know, an egg is a lot of work," Appa said. "Who will keep it warm when you go to sleep?"

Hazel said, "It will stay in my bed." But Twig began to cry, so Hazel said, "OK, it can stay in Twig's cradle half the night."

"Who will move it from Twig's cradle to your bed?" Appa asked.

"You and Umma can do that," Hazel said. "I will be asleep."

"Oh, I see," Appa said.

"What about when the egg hatches?" Appa asked.

"We will build it a nest!" said Hazel. "Twig will fetch the worms, and I will teach it to fly."

"You've thought of almost everything," Appa said.

Now the sun was warming the egg, and the mouse family, too.

"Have you thought of what you'll name the chick?" asked Appa.

"Not yet," said Hazel.

"Before Twig was born, you wanted to name her Toad," said Appa.

Hazel giggled. "I am glad you didn't call her that."

She thought for a moment. "I know! We will name our chick . . . Dandelion! Twig, what do you think?"

But Twig didn't answer.

"Where is Twig?" Hazel squeaked. Hazel and Appa looked all around, but they did not see her.

Twig!

Then Hazel spotted Twig's tail.

"I thought you were lost!" Hazel cried.

"She *was* lost," Appa said. "But only for a moment. She's lucky you found her!"

Hazel was very quiet. Then she asked, "Appa, do you think Dandelion is lost? Just like Twig was?"

"Yes," Appa said. "It is definitely a Lost Egg."

"Then I think we have to help it find its own nest," Hazel said.

"We will," Appa said. "And I am proud of you for being such a thoughtful mouse."

Appa fetched Umma and her ladder, and they all started looking for the egg's home.

"There are three eggs in this nest!" Umma called down. "They are white with speckles."

"No," Hazel called back. "Dandelion is pale blue with no speckles."

"This nest is small," Umma said. "The eggs inside are tiny."
Hazel looked at their egg. "No, Dandelion is big!" she called up.

Umma climbed tree after tree. They found eggs that were brown, white, and blue. Speckled and unspeckled. Big and small.

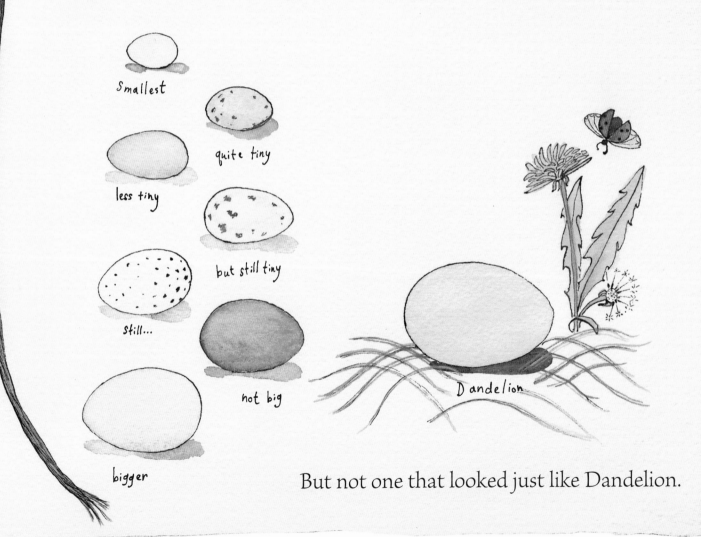

Smallest

quite tiny

less tiny

but still tiny

Still...

not big

bigger

Dandelion

But not one that looked just like Dandelion.

Hazel began to worry they'd never find the right nest for a big, pale blue egg with no speckles. But then she heard a quack down among the daffodils. Which made Hazel think: *Some birds live up in trees. But some birds live . . .*

"Quack!" Hazel called out. Twig tried to quack, too.

A pair of very worried ducks burst out of the daffodils,
followed by one tiny duckling. When they saw Dandelion,
they flapped their wings and quacked with joy.

"Oh, Dandelion," said Hazel. "I am glad you are a Found Egg now." She hugged the egg and ducks goodbye.

But as the mouse family turned to go, they all heard a new sound: *Creak . . . crack.*

"Dandelion!" said Hazel.

Hazel and Twig and the ducklings played. The ducklings
followed Hazel and Twig. Hazel and Twig followed the
ducklings.

Then they said goodbye, and Hazel and Twig followed
Umma and Appa home through the mouse-high grass and
golden afternoon.

"It is sad we did not get to take Dandelion home," Hazel said to Twig as they trailed along behind. "But she has her own sister now. Just like you have me . . .

and I have you."

Illustration facing "Umma climbed tree after tree" and bugs throughout the book are inspired by the works of eighteenth-century naturalist James Bolton in the collection of the Yale Center for British Art.

First edition 2020

Library of Congress Catalog Card Number pending
ISBN 978-1-5362-0492-6

19 20 21 22 23 24 LEO 10 9 8 7 6 5 4 3 2 1

Printed in Heshan, Guangdong, China

This book was typeset in Brioso Pro.
The illustrations were done in ink and watercolor.

Candlewick Press
99 Dover Street
Somerville, Massachusetts 02144

visit us at www.candlewick.com